MINECRAFT

Farshore

First published in the United States by Random House Children's Books
and in Canada by Penguin Random House Canada Limited.

First published in Great Britain in 2021 by Farshore
An imprint of HarperCollins*Publishers*
1 London Bridge Street, London SE1 9GF
www.farshore.co.uk

HarperCollins*Publishers*
1st Floor, Watermarque Building, Ringsend Road
Dublin 4, Ireland

Written by Nick Eliopulos
Illustrated by Alan Batson and Chris Hill

ISBN 978 0 7555 0321 6

Printed in the United Kingdom

001

Stay safe online. Farshore is not responsible for content hosted by third parties.
Farshore takes its responsibility to the planet and its inhabitants very seriously.
We aim to use papers from well-managed forests run by responsible suppliers.

MINECRAFT

THE STONESWORD SAGA

CRACK IN THE CODE

MORGAN

HARPER

PLAYERS!

PO

JODI

THEO

PROLOGUE

Theo Grayson stood alone in the Overworld.

He wasn't supposed to be here by himself. It was one of his friends' most important rules. **Nobody went into Minecraft alone.**

There were monsters out there, after all. And he and his friends had souped-up goggles that let them actually enter the game for real. And that meant the monsters, the danger – and the *unknown* – were real.

But today, curiosity had its hooks in him. He was here looking for something. Something new. **Something . . . unusual.**

Theo saw all the most common mobs of Minecraft. He saw chickens and sheep. He saw pigs and cows.

And then he saw something colourful out of the corner of his eye.

Theo's digital avatar didn't have a heartbeat, but he felt like his pulse was racing. His avatar didn't have lungs, but he felt like he was holding his breath. He spun around and looked to the sky.

There, fluttering in the air, was a single butterfly.

"I've done it," Theo said out loud, even though he was alone. **"I'VE CREATED A NEW MOB!"**

He hoped his friends would be impressed. He hoped they wouldn't be mad – even though he had broken a second rule that day.

He wasn't supposed to mess with the code.

But that was one rule he didn't agree with.

He was just doing a little modding.

What was the worst that could happen?

Chapter 1

THE MORE THINGS CHANGE, THE MORE THEY . . . NO. WAIT. THIS IS GOING TO BE TOTALLY DIFFERENT.

Theo arrived early at Woodsword Middle School. For once, he was eager to start the day.

After all, he had news to share with his friends. Big news.

Big **Minecraft**-related news.

Theo was the newest member of an unofficial Minecraft club. On most days, the club met after school in Woodsword's computer lab, where they played Minecraft together on a shared server.

But Theo couldn't wait until after school. **He needed to find**

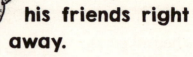

his friends right away.

He hurried to the large oak tree where the group sometimes gathered before school. Today, only one figure stood beneath the tree. She wore a fedora and dark sunglasses. Despite the disguise, Theo recognised Jodi Mercado immediately.

"Hi, Jodi," he said. "Do you have a minute?"

"Jodi? Who's Jodi?" said Jodi. **"I'm Agent J. I don't know any Jodi!"**

"Oh," said Theo. "My mistake." What could he do but play along?

After a few moments of uncomfortable silence, Agent J lowered her sunglasses and whispered, "Just kidding, it's me. Jodi! But be cool – **I'm on a deep-cover surveillance mission."**

She leaned against the tree trunk and peered around it. Theo peeked, too, but he didn't see anything of interest. A few students had gathered on the lawn. Safety patrols watched over the crossing. The public library stood across the street.

"What are we looking at, uh, Agent J?" Theo asked.

"Doc took a bunch of equipment into the library precisely" – Jodi glanced her watch – "four minutes and forty-two seconds ago. *High-tech* equipment."

"Is that unusual?" Theo asked. "Doc" was **Dr Culpepper, their science teacher.** Theo knew she liked to tinker with technology . . . and that her tinkering often caused trouble. Her inventions and upgrades had a way of turning out not quite the way she planned.

"Everything Doc *does* is unusual," Jodi answered. "Maybe moving that equipment is harmless. Maybe it's nothing!"

"Yeah," said Theo. "You're probably—"

"Then again, *maybe* she's replacing the local librarians with cyborgs. **Once the cyborgs are in charge of the library, they'll control all the information.** And once they control the information, they'll control the world. Just think of the overdue fees they'll charge, Theo! Those fees will be astronomical!"

"Sure," Theo said. "Maybe that's it. Or maybe she's just donating old equipment. Or upgrading their air-conditioning. Or—"

"Hold that thought!" said Jodi, interrupting him. **"There she is."**

Theo looked again, and he saw that Jodi was right. Doc was in the crossing, heading back onto school property.

"I need to follow her. Sorry, Theo."

Theo shrugged. "Do what you have to do. But where's everybody else?"

"Dunno," said Jodi as she ducked behind a nearby bush. "I think Po is in the gym this morning. Check there!"

Po Chen was in the gymnasium, just like Jodi had said. As Theo watched, Po sped across the basketball court, turned his wheelchair on a dime, lined up a shot and sent the ball sailing towards the basket. *Swish!* It was nothing but net.

Theo didn't know much about sports, but

it was easy to see why Po was a star player. Woodsword's basketball team was a mixed ability team, which meant that every player used a wheelchair during games, even though some of them didn't use wheelchairs in everyday life. It took a lot of practice – and somehow Po still had time for other extracurriculars, too. Including the after-school Minecraft club.

Theo thought that waking up early to practise sports *before* school sounded like way too much work. He could barely get out of bed in time for breakfast. **He yawned and almost got hit by a stray basketball!**

"Sorry, Theo!" said Po as he wheeled to the edge of the court. "That was a terrible pass. I almost turned basketball into dodgeball!"

"No problem," said Theo. He retrieved the ball from beneath the stands. "I wanted to talk to you anyway," he said, handing Po the ball and lowering his voice. **"About Minecraft, and — the Evoker King."**

Po's jaw dropped. That had gotten his attention.

"Hurry up, Po!" said a teammate.

"Get back here!" said another. "You obviously need the practice."

"Ooh, burn!" said Po, smiling. "I'll show you who needs practice!" He turned back to Theo. "Sorry, man. Can it wait?"

"Sure," said Theo, frowning a little. "Do you know where the others are?"

"I know Harper had something to do in the science lab. Look for her there!"

Harper Houston was right in the middle of an extra-credit experiment. That was how she liked to use her morning time. With a pipette, she dripped liquid into a beaker, drop by drop. She spied Theo out of the corner of her eye.

"Sorry, Theo," said Harper. "I can't talk right this second. **If I lose my concentration here** even a little, the results could be ..."

"Explosive?" Theo asked with a little too much enthusiasm. His favourite science projects involved rockets and volcanos and soda geysers.

"Well, no," said Harper. "I'm not working on anything dangerous. But if I get the measurements wrong, **it could make this whole wing of the school smell like skunk!** And nobody needs that right now."

Theo took a step back. "You've convinced me," he said. "I definitely won't distract you . . . with my news about the artificial intelligence who's been living in our Minecraft game."

Harper's eyes went wide behind her protective goggles. "Theo, you rascal! If anything can distract me, it's that. And you know it!"

He did know it. Harper was one of the smartest people Theo knew . . . and one of the most curious. She idolised Doc, loved science and cared deeply about conservation and ecology.

She also had a great mind for Minecraft. Harper seemed to have every crafting formula and potion recipe committed to memory. Of *course* she would be interested in news about the artificial intelligence they called the Evoker King.

But Theo really didn't want to be responsible for stinking up the school first thing in the morning.

"Sorry, sorry," he said, grinning. "I'll fill you in later. **I'm going to try to find Morgan before the bell rings.**"

"Check the cafe," Harper said. "I think he had studying to do."

Morgan Mercado didn't even look up from his textbook when Theo approached his table.

"Not now, Theo," Morgan said. "I'm sorry, but I've got a test that I am *not* prepared for."

"No problem," Theo said. But he couldn't keep the disappointment out of his voice. **This was not how he'd imagined the morning going.** How were all of his friends this busy so early in the day?

Morgan seemed to realise Theo was hurt. He sighed and looked up from his book. "Is it something important?"

"Sort of," Theo said. **"It's about the Evoker King, but I can tell you later."**

Morgan slammed his book shut and leaned forward. "Why didn't you say so in the first place?" he asked.

Theo grinned. He should have realised: Morgan *always* had time for Minecraft.

"I've been studying the code," Theo said. "And learning everything I can about mods. You know what those are, right?"

"Sort of," Morgan said. **"I know 'mod' is short for 'modification,' and 'modification' means 'change.' That's what you call it when someone makes changes to a game's code."**

"You're mostly right," said Theo. "Only, a mod

doesn't make changes to the *actual game code.* It's more like it puts extra code on top of the game code. Minecraft mods will do things like create new blocks or weapons or gems. They don't technically mess with how the game works. But they can make the game different in little ways."

Morgan nodded. **The Minecraft version that he and his friends had been playing was more than a little different.** It was uniquely weird. That was because Doc had used the school computers to experiment with virtual reality and artificial intelligence. So when Theo, Morgan and the others played Minecraft . . . they played from *inside* the game. **Their minds were transported to a living, breathing world that was wondrous . . . but it also gave Survival Mode a totally new meaning!**

And they weren't alone in that world — artificial intelligence lived inside the game. He called himself the Evoker King. He had been their enemy, then their friend . . . and now he was in need of a rescue.

For reasons none of them understood, the Evoker King had turned to stone. He was a lifeless statue: Unmoving. Unfeeling. Unthinking.

It was a problem that Theo was determined to solve.

"Have you been trying to help the Evoker King?" Morgan asked. "Is that why you're learning about mods?"

"Yeah, exactly." Theo nodded. "Mods are how Doc affected the game. **That means it's a mod that gave the Evoker King access to Minecraft in the first place.** So I've been making my own mods. I've been practising. *Experimenting.* So that I can figure out what went wrong with the Evoker King. So that I can fix him!"

He waited for Morgan to crack a smile. But Morgan looked deeply serious. "I don't know if this is a good idea, Theo," he said at last. "Messing with that stuff sounds risky. What if you make the problem worse?"

Theo wasn't sure what to say to that. He had thought Morgan would be thrilled with his idea.

"We should talk about this later," Morgan said. "I really do have to study."

"Okay," said Theo.

"And, Theo," said Morgan. **"Don't go messing with anything before we talk. Don't make any new mods and don't make any changes to old ones.** Okay? This should be a team discussion."

"Yeah. Right," said Theo. "Of course. Team discussion."

But Theo knew it was too late for that. He'd created several mods already. And he'd started

tinkering with Doc's code. **He had done it without telling anybody what he was doing.** Morgan wasn't going to be happy.

Theo decided not to say anything more. He hoped his blushing didn't give him away. But luckily, Morgan had already turned back to his book.

Later in the day, Theo met up with the others. They gathered outside the computer lab, as they did most days.

After school was *their* time. To play Minecraft together. To share adventures and build great things.

But this was not a day like any other.

Morgan threw open the doors of the computer lab . . . and they all gasped at what they saw.

"What in the world happened?!" said Po.

In unison, Harper and Jodi said, "The computers . . ."

"They're gone!" Theo finished.

Chapter 2

NOT IN MY COMPUTER LAB, BUTTERFLY . . . IF THAT IS YOUR REAL NAME!

Morgan was stunned. He couldn't speak. He couldn't move. **He felt like his brain couldn't process what his eyes were seeing.**

The computer lab was his favourite place. It was like a clubhouse – the one spot where he could forget about homework and chores and just spend time with his friends, gaming, laughing, sharing Minecraft adventures.

And now **the computer lab was gone** – replaced by some sort of indoor jungle. Bright green leaves were everywhere, and the air was warm and wet. A rainforest might as well have sprouted up in the middle of the classroom!

Were they in the wrong room? Were they at the wrong school? Were they on the wrong *planet*? Just what was going on here?

"Where did all these plants come from?" asked Jodi. She craned her neck for a better look and twirled in a slow circle.

"Well, they're potted plants," said Harper. She pushed a leaf aside for a better view. "They didn't just grow out of the ground. So someone brought them here."

"Did they bring the cocoons, too?" asked Po.

"Cocoons?" echoed Jodi. "Where?"

Po wheeled over to one of the plants and pointed out a small cocoon. Then another, and another. Now that Morgan knew what to look for, he saw them everywhere! They were hanging from leaves and light fixtures and windowsills.

"They're butterfly cocoons," said Harper. "From several different species, I think."

"This has to be Doc's latest mad-science experiment!" said Jodi.

"I knew we would be learning about butterflies in class this week," said Theo. "But this is overkill, even for Doc." Fascinated, he stuck out a finger to poke a cocoon.

"Careful!" said Harper. "They're fragile."

Theo poked the cocoon anyway. "You know, there are thousands of species of moths and

butterflies in the world. I don't think there'd be so many if they were *that* delicate."

Normally, Morgan would tell Theo to cut it out. But he was still reeling with shock. "I don't understand this at all," he said. He dropped to a sitting position, right on the ground, and put his head in his hands. **"Where did all the computers go?"**

Jodi snapped her fingers. "The public library!" she said. "This morning, I saw Doc taking equipment over there. She must have relocated the computers."

"Including the server we use to play Minecraft," said Theo. **"And the VR goggles — they're gone, too."**

"We should go across the street and see for

ourselves," said Po. "We can go right now!"

Morgan felt a little better now that he knew where the computers had gone. He sometimes teased his sister when she acted like a spy, but she *was* good at noticing things that other people missed. "Jodi and I should call our parents first," he said. "We need permission to leave school grounds."

Harper took out her smartphone. She was the only one of them who had one. "We can all take turns calling our parents," she said, handing the phone to Morgan first. "But hurry. I want answers as soon as possible!"

Morgan agreed with that, one hundred per cent.

Excalibur County Library and Media Centre was a large concrete building right across the street from Woodsword Middle School. Morgan had come here with his family almost every weekend when he was younger. They would go to story times and puppet shows and leave with stacks of picture books.

And no visit to the library was complete without a quick stop at the statue out front. It was Morgan's favourite kind of statue – one you were

allowed to touch! It was a model of a sword in a stone, just like the famous Excalibur of Arthurian legend. Because of the statue, and because Excalibur County Library and Media Centre was such a mouthful, kids had always just called the place **Stonesword Library.**

Morgan touched the statue for good luck as he walked past.

As soon as they stepped inside, they saw two familiar figures standing in the lobby.

Ms Minerva, their homeroom teacher, was talking with their science teacher, Dr Culpepper. They were Morgan's favourite teachers, but they didn't always see eye to eye. In fact, Morgan quickly realised, they were having an argument right now.

"Absolutely not, Doc!" said Ms Minerva. "Not here. **The library is my happy place!**"

"I only want to make it happier!" said Doc. "Don't be so afraid of progress, Minerva."

Morgan desperately wanted to run up and ask Doc what was going on with the computer lab. Ms Minerva might know, too. She was the only adult who knew all about the Evoker King, and **she had even helped them on some of their Minecraft adventures.** For a grown-up, she was a whiz at gathering resources.

But Morgan knew better than to interrupt when adults were in the middle of whatever it was that adults found to get so upset about.

"You've already turned Woodsword into your own personal high-tech wonderland," Ms Minerva

said to Doc. "The lockers are secured with biometric locks, the overhead lights are controlled by whistling **and the coffee maker chats about the weather while it brews."** Ms Minerva rubbed her temples. "And the coffee isn't even very good!"

"Those are all wonderful innovations," Doc argued. **"I refuse to apologise for making Woodsword the most technologically advanced school in the district.** And I certainly won't apologise about the coffee. Coffee always tastes terrible, and you drink too much of it. How many cups did you have today?" Doc leaned forward and sniffed loudly. "I smell at least five cups on your breath."

Ms Minerva gasped. **"How dare you?!"**

Beside Morgan, Theo chuckled. "Wow, this is entertaining," he said. "I should have brought some popcorn."

Morgan didn't think it was funny, though. Watching the teachers argue made him feel anxious.

"You forgot to sign in," said a voice. Morgan turned to see a man holding a clipboard. He was an adult, but obviously younger than the teachers. He wore colourful sneakers that matched his necktie.

For a moment, Morgan worried that they were in trouble. But the man smiled as he handed Morgan the clipboard. "You're Woodsword students, right? Just sign in here, and then you're free to explore."

"Thanks," Morgan said, signing his name to the sheet. **"I've never been here without my parents."**

"And we haven't been here at all in at least a year," said Jodi. "We mostly use the school library these days."

The man's eyes went wide. "Then you'll need the

tour. A lot has changed here in the last year." **He took the clipboard back when they'd all signed it, and he shook it gently.** "*This* will have to change next. I mean, a sign-in sheet for the computer room on a clipboard just feels so old-fashioned, don't you agree? Hopefully Doc can help us with that."

"Does Doc work here?" asked Harper.

"Not officially," said the librarian. "But she's helping us upgrade some of our equipment."

Morgan snuck a look at Doc. She and Ms Minerva were still in the lobby, waving their arms in the air as they talked loudly.

"Someone should probably shush them," said the man. "But I'm not that kind of librarian." He smiled. **"My name is Mr Malory.** I'm the new media specialist. Let me show you around."

Mr Malory took them on a brief tour. Morgan thought he knew what to expect — books, and a lot of them. But there were also vinyl records, DVDs and even video games!

Harper ran ahead to look at a bulky electronic object. "Is this a 3D printer?" she asked.

"It is!" said Mr Malory. "You'll be using it for some of your STEM projects this year. And look over here." He pointed through a large window, into a room where a teenager with a VR helmet sat at a computer with a steering wheel attached to it. "This is our driver's education room. We only have one device so far, but I hope to expand it."

Po made a high-pitched sound of pure joy. **"VR can teach me how to drive? Sign me up!"**

Mr Malory chuckled. "Not until you're older, I'm afraid. That room is strictly for teens."

Jodi grinned at Po. "By the time we're teenagers, they'll probably be able to beam the driver's manual directly into our brains."

"You might be right," said Mr Malory. **"Technology is changing at a rapid pace.** And educators like me need to keep up with those changes."

"I couldn't have said it better myself," said a familiar voice. Doc approached the group, grinning from ear to ear. "Mr Malory and I are going to bring this building into the twenty-first century!"

"There's nothing wrong with this place as it is," said Ms Minerva, who trailed behind Doc. "And there isn't enough space to make all the changes you want to make."

"There will be plenty of room if we digitise more of the books," said Doc. She waved an electronic tablet under Ms Minerva's nose. **"I have a whole library's worth of books on this tiny device!** There's no reason to have shelves and shelves of books taking up space."

"There is every reason in the world to make room for books," said Ms Minerva. "*Especially* in a library." She closed her eyes and took a big, deep breath. "For one thing, a library should smell like books. I love that smell. Don't you?"

Doc took a sniff of the air . . . and promptly sneezed into her sleeve. "I'm allergic to dust," she said.

Mr Malory stepped forward. "Don't worry, Ms Minerva," he said. **"The books aren't going anywhere."**

Ms Minerva nodded. "That's all I wanted to

hear. I know I can trust you to keep Stonesword special." She turned to the kids. "Mr Malory here was my student not too many years ago. I had a feeling he would grow up to be a librarian."

Mr Malory cleared his throat. "Technically, I'm a media specialist."

Ms Minerva grinned at the kids. "I've always preferred to be called a 'librarian,' personally."

Morgan grinned back. When Ms Minerva played Minecraft, she wore a modified villager skin and called herself the Librarian.

"That reminds me. I think I know which technological innovation these students are looking for," said Ms Minerva. And she pulled a familiar VR headset from her duffle bag.

Morgan felt a rush of relief. **That VR headset wasn't just an average piece of equipment.** Doc had upgraded it with cutting-edge technology. **There were**

only six of them in the entire world!

"I'm so glad to see this," Morgan said, taking the headset as soon as Ms Minerva offered it to him.

"I almost forgot in all the excitement," said Jodi. **"But what exactly happened to the computer lab?"**

Ms Minerva raised an eyebrow and looked at Doc. "Yes, Doc," she said. "Why don't you fill us in?"

"Okay, so, technically, that's my fault," said Doc. "I left the lid off a terrarium over the weekend."

"Right," said Po, tapping his chin. "The terrarium. It all makes sense now." He leaned over to Harper and whispered, **"What's a terrarium?"**

"It's like an aquarium," Harper said. "But without the water."

"Right you are," said Doc. "And this particular terrarium was full of caterpillars. The little things escaped and got *everywhere.*"

"Doc didn't want to disturb the caterpillars – especially when they started spinning their cocoons," said Mr Malory. "So she asked if she could move the computers here. Now Woodsword has its very own butterfly sanctuary, and **Stonesword will be hosting a few of Doc's classes and after-school activities."**

"I hope you know what you're in for," said Ms Minerva. "Doc is brilliant. But chaos follows wherever she goes."

"That's unkind, Minerva," said Doc. "You shouldn't say such things in front of Mr Malory."

"It's the truth!" said Ms Minerva. "Or did you miss the morning announcements today, when your AI newscaster gave advice on how to make bigger, wetter spitballs?"

"It's news the kids care about!" Doc replied defensively.

"I can't listen to any more of this," said Ms Minerva. **She handed the duffle bag of headsets to Morgan and stormed out.** "I need a *real* cup of coffee."

"We're not done . . . discussing!" said Doc, running after her.

Mr Malory sighed.

"Maybe I should have shushed them after all,"

he said with a mischievous grin.

"They disagree a lot," said Jodi. "But that felt especially intense."

Morgan gripped his headset to his chest. "Mr Malory?" he asked. "Are we allowed to use the computers from the Woodsword computer lab?"

"Of course," said the media specialist. "Doc has everything set up and ready to go."

Morgan breathed a sigh of relief. **It felt like everything around him was changing faster than he could handle.**

But there was one place they could go where everything made sense: **Minecraft!**

Chapter 3

THAT FEELING WHEN A PRETTY GOOD PLAN GOES TERRIBLY, TERRIBLY WRONG . . .

Jodi always felt a thrill when she opened her eyes and saw Minecraft's Overworld spread out before her in glorious 3D. It was just as real as the real world – a virtual space that she could *touch*.

But there was a twinge of disappointment this time, too. Because she saw the rolling hills, blocky trees, swaying flowers and shining square of sun . . . but she didn't see her friend Ash.

Ash Kapoor was an important part of their Minecraft squad. She was a scout, a natural leader and a good listener. Things hadn't been quite the same since she'd moved away.

They kept in touch. Ash had even taken the

sixth headset with her so she could join them in the game world from time to time. But they'd had a hard time making that happen. Ash was busy in her new home, and her school wasn't on the same schedule as Woodsword.

Jodi missed her friend.

"What's that over there?" Harper asked. "Is that a camel?"

"You'd better get your vision checked, Harper," Po said, teasing. "I'm not a camel. I'm a butterfly!"

Po liked to change his avatar's skin every few days. Today, in honour of the cocoons in the old computer lab, he was trying out a butterfly skin.

But Harper hadn't been talking about Po. "Not

you," she said. "Up there, on the hill. Look!"

Jodi turned to see what Harper had spotted. **It was a huge, animal-shaped concrete sculpture atop the nearest hill.** A small stream of water fell from its mouth to form a river in the grass. Jodi recognised Ash's handiwork immediately.

"IT'S A LLAMA," Jodi said, smiling. "It's even sort of spitting like a llama, see?"

"It looks more like it's drooling," said Po.

"Still, it's pretty cool," said Morgan. "Ash must have made that." He turned to Jodi. "It's her way of saying hi to you, Jodi. She knows how much you love llamas."

Jodi's heart swelled. It was the best sorry-I-missed-you present she could imagine.

Theo, on the other hand, was too occupied with Evoker King to even look at the statue. "I can't believe it," he said glumly. "The Evoker King is *still* solid stone."

Jodi looked the Evoker King over from top to bottom. Theo was right. The King hadn't changed at all. He hadn't moved an inch since the day he'd turned to stone. They were no closer to understanding what had happened to him, or why.

"WELL, HE HAS TO CHANGE BACK EVENTUALLY," said Po. "Doesn't he?"

Harper shrugged her blocky shoulders. "It's impossible to say. We just don't have enough data."

"Well, we can't stay here much longer," said Morgan. "We've been in this spot for ages, hoping that whatever happened to E.K. is temporary."

Po realised that Morgan was right. **They'd been spawning in the same area for a while, afraid of leaving the Evoker King behind.** Of course, they'd still had plenty of fun. Po got to try out new skins and role-play different characters. Jodi got to make sculptures. Harper was happy as long as they had materials to mine, and Morgan was happy as long as there were hostile mobs to fight.

The monstrous mobs were endless. They always appeared when the sun went down. But Po and his friends were having a harder time finding good materials in the caverns below their feet. They had mined most of the good stuff. All that was left in the area was stone and dirt.

"I think it's time to go," said Harper. "If we want to gather new resources, we need to move on."

Jodi's jaw dropped. **"BUT WE CAN'T LEAVE HIM!"** she said. "We had *just* convinced him to be our friend. How would he feel if he woke up and realised we had abandoned him?"

Harper rubbed her chin. "Okay. So what if we take him with us?" she suggested.

Po made a show of trying to push the Evoker King over. **"HE'S REALLY HEAVY,"** he said.

"Hm." Theo squinted. "Stuff in Minecraft doesn't really have *weight,* though. So how can he be heavy?" He poked the statue. "I think it's more likely that he's fixed in place. He's part of the scenery now. But maybe we could move him . . ."

"**WITH A SILK TOUCH TOOL!**" said Morgan.

"What's that?" asked Jodi.

"It's an enchantment," her brother answered in his geeking-out voice. "If you enchant a tool with Silk Touch, you can remove a fixed item without breaking it. **YOU SORT OF JUST . . . KNOCK IT LOOSE.**" He turned to Harper and Po. "What do you two think?"

"I think it's worth a try," said Harper.

"The Evoker King should fly free," Po said, dramatically fluttering his digital wings. "Like me!"

Morgan rolled his square eyes at Po's butterfly voice, but Jodi giggled.

"So we'll craft a Silk Touch pickaxe so we can move him," said Theo. "Then we can put him on a mine cart, lay down some rails and take him to our next base of operations."

"I like it!" said Jodi. "Good plan, Theo."

Theo smiled brightly. "Thanks."

"We should have everything we need for the enchantment," said Harper. She ran into the small building where they kept their beds and their chests full of resources. **They called it the Shack.** When she came back, she set an enchanting table down on the grass and held out a shining blue rock. "I was hoping we'd find a good use for this lapis lazuli."

"Ooh, pretty," said Jodi.

"Pretty . . . and powerful," said Harper. **"LAPIS LAZULI CAN PROVIDE THE ENERGY NEEDED FOR AN ENCHANTMENT."**

Morgan set a smelter next to the enchanting table. "We've mined a lot of iron ore lately," he said. "We should smelt it all into ingots. We'll need those for the mine cart and rails."

"I'll go get the ore," Po said, fluttering into the Shack.

"And I'll provide the pickaxe," said Theo. He held out an iron tool. "Here you go, Harper. Go ahead and work your magic."

It only took a moment. Harper fed the blue lapis to the enchanting table. **There was a burst**

of light, and Theo's pickaxe shone with the power of the enchantment.

"I guess I'll do the honours," Theo said. He approached the Evoker King. He gripped his pickaxe, lifted it above his head . . . and swung.

Where the pickaxe struck the stone, **a crack appeared.**

"Stop!" said Morgan.

"That doesn't look good," said Jodi.

Theo took a step back. His eyes were fixed on the Evoker King, and on the small crack in his stony skin.

As they watched, **that crack began to grow.** And glow . . .

Chapter 4

DON'T BUILD WALLS BETWEEN YOU AND YOUR FRIENDS. DO BUILD WALLS BETWEEN YOU AND HOSTILE MOBS OF UNKNOWN ORIGIN.

Po stepped out of the Shack in time to see the Evoker King splitting apart.

Po was usually quick with a joke. He didn't take many things seriously. **Even when Minecraft got scary, he usually remembered that it was a game.**

But this wasn't funny. What if the Evoker King crumbled to dust before their very eyes? What if their new friend was just . . . shattered?

Broken?

Destroyed?

Po had to do something!

He crossed the grass in a hurry. Then he

wrapped his arms around the Evoker King's stony surface. Maybe if he squeezed tightly enough, he could hold him together.

Maybe not.

There was a great flash of light and a sound like breaking pottery. Po flew backward – wings and all – and crashed into his friends. They tumbled to the ground in a heap.

When Po lifted his head off the ground, the air was thick with curls of smoke and something bright and colourful, flickering and flitting. **Butterflies?** There weren't supposed to be butterflies in Minecraft, but Po could swear he saw them fluttering through the smoke.

Maybe he just had butterflies on the brain.

He strained his eyes. Just barely, he could see something else moving in the smoke. Something much bigger than a butterfly . . .

"Is . . . is that you, **E.K.?**" he asked.

There was no answer except a low growl.

"That sure didn't sound like him," said Morgan.

Po still couldn't make out many details through the smoke and dust. **Was that . . . a wing? A huge rocky fist? A pig snout?**

Something was very, very wrong here.

Po started laying down a row of blocks. Stone, dirt, brick – anything and everything he had in his inventory.

"WALL. NOW!" he shouted.

Harper quickly joined him. They didn't stop until there was a low wall between them and . . .

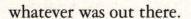

whatever was out there.

"What did you see?" asked Morgan. Po just hushed him.

They all waited in silence for a long minute.

They heard grunting and growling and a series of wet snorts. Then they heard flapping wings and trudging feet. All the sounds began to get farther away. Finally, there was silence. Po waited another minute before he poked his head above the wall.

There was nothing there. Just a crater where the Evoker King had once stood.

"What in the world was *that*?!" Jodi cried,

leaving the safety of the wall to peer into the crater.

"That shouldn't have been possible," said Harper. **"I GOT THE ENCHANTMENT RIGHT ... I KNOW I DID."**

"Maybe someone else should take this thing," Theo said, setting down the glowing pickaxe. "I feel sick."

"I don't understand what happened," Po said. He looked around. "Did the Evoker King just explode? Is he . . . gone? Forever?"

"Maybe not," said Jodi. **"LOOK OVER HERE. FOOTPRINTS!"**

Po saw what she meant. There was a line of little squares leading away from the crater, across the grass and into the nearby forest. Those squares looked like small, blocky footsteps.

Morgan seemed suspicious. "Since when are there footprints in Minecraft?"

"Well, I can explain that one, at least," Theo said. He snuck a guilty look at Morgan. "It's a mod."

"DOC MADE A FOOTPRINT MOD?" said Po. "Why haven't we noticed it before now?"

"It's not one of Doc's," Theo said. **"IT'S ONE OF MINE."**

Morgan frowned. "I thought I told you not to add any new mods," he said.

"But I did this before you said that," Theo said quickly. "And this mod is harmless. And helpful!" He smiled. "I did it for Ash. This way, if we ever leave our Shack without her, she can just follow our footprints to find us."

"Sure," said Morgan. "But what else might follow our footprints? What if this mod leads monsters right to us?"

Theo's smile evaporated. "I don't think that will happen."

"You don't *think* so," said Morgan. "But that's the point. You aren't sure. You're being reckless!"

"Morgan," said Jodi. "Don't be mean."

"I'm not being mean!" Morgan argued. "Unlike Theo, *I'm* being a team player. When you're on a team, you talk about this stuff before you do it." He turned to face Theo. "Okay, Theo? **YOU CAN'T JUST DO WHATEVER YOU WANT TO DO, BECAUSE IT AFFECTS US ALL.**"

Theo looked like he wanted to shrink away into nothing. The blocky shoulders of his avatar

drooped. "Sorry, Morgan," he said. "I'll be more careful in the future."

That seemed good enough for Morgan. He let the conversation end there.

But Po couldn't help wondering about something. Theo had said, **"IT'S ONE OF MINE."**

One of them?

Did that mean Theo had installed more mods? **Was their game of Minecraft about to get even stranger?**

Chapter 5

JOIN THE DEFENSIVE CIRCLE TODAY! YOU'LL BE GLAD YOU DID.

Harper led the way into the forest. She let the footprints guide her.

"Evoker King?" cried Jodi, creeping along behind her. **"ARE YOU OUT HERE, EVOKER KING?"**

"Man, that name is a mouthful," said Po. "When we find him, we should really suggest something a little easier. Like Bob!"

"I don't think we should be shouting *anything* right now," said Morgan. "It's dark under these trees. Something dangerous could spawn here."

"We might be *following* something dangerous," Harper added. "If these are the Evoker King's tracks . . . **IF HE SURVIVED WHATEVER HAPPENED BACK THERE** . . . why would he have come this way? Why avoid us?"

"Yeah. Hope for the best," Theo said. He pulled a splash potion from his inventory. "But be prepared for anything."

Harper certainly hoped they would find the Evoker King. **He was an AI so advanced that he had emotions and he loved Minecraft as much as Harper and her friends did!** Her mind reeled thinking about how much they could learn from him, if only they got the chance.

As they walked on, Harper noticed something strange. A block of wood was missing from a nearby tree's trunk. A minute later, she saw the missing block of wood on the ground ahead. Based on the footprints, whoever they were following had moved that block of wood.

And now she saw similar signs all along the path: **A block of dirt missing from the ground.** A block of spruce wood stuck onto an oak tree. The signs appeared completely random.

While she wondered about that, Harper spotted a butterfly flitting between the trees. It took her a moment to realise – **there were no butterflies in Minecraft.**

She looked back at where it had been. There was nothing there.

Maybe Po was right. Maybe she needed to get her eyes checked.

The trees parted, revealing a clearing in the forest. Clouds had moved in to cover the square sun, making the light dim, but Harper could see a figure standing on the far side of the clearing. **It was tall and blocky, and it seemed to be stacking blocks.**

"I think that's him," Jodi said.

"It looks like him," Harper agreed. She felt a rush of hope, and cried out, **"EVOKER KING! HELLO? OVER HERE!"**

The figure paused at the sound of her voice. It turned to look at them.

"That's not the Evoker King," said Morgan. "That's an enderman. Harper, don't look!"

Too late. Harper turned her head, but the enderman had seen her staring.

And endermen *hated* to be stared at.

The mob emitted a low, terrifying shriek. Harper risked taking another look – but it was gone.

"IT'S TELEPORTING!" she said, and as soon as the warning left her mouth, the enderman appeared right in the middle of their group! With a wave of its long arm, it sent Harper stumbling backward. Then it swung at the others. Jodi and Morgan were both hit.

"OH NO, YOU DON'T!" said Po, and he readied his weapon. If it weren't such a serious moment,

Harper would have laughed at the sight of a butterfly armed with a sword. Funny or not, Po's attack was useless. The enderman teleported away again, and Po's sword swept through empty air.

"IT'S FAST," said Po.

"Unusually fast," said Morgan. Then the enderman appeared right behind him, striking him again before blinking away.

"Ow!" said Morgan. He looked around the clearing, frantic. "I don't think I can take many more hits like that one."

"Everyone, clump up!" said Harper. "Put your backs together so it can't sneak behind us."

"No, we should go on the offensive!" said Theo. **"I'VE FOUGHT PLENTY OF ENDERMEN BEFORE."**

Po and Morgan joined Harper. They drew their weapons and stood back to back. **Fighting mobs was not Jodi's preferred way of experiencing Minecraft,** but she knew a good idea when she heard it. She quickly joined them in the defensive circle.

Theo, however, stood alone.

"Don't be careless," said Po.

"Theo," Jodi hissed to get his attention.

"Get over here," said Harper.

Thunder rumbled overhead. Suddenly, the enderman reappeared right in front of Harper.

She slashed with her sword, and its eyes flashed—

And her sword disappeared.

"What was that?" she said, shocked. "Did it just teleport my sword away?"

"Don't worry," said Theo. **"I'VE GOT THE ENDERMAN IN MY SIGHTS!"**

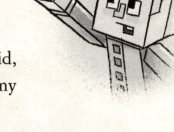

Theo lobbed his splash potion at the mob, which quickly blinked away – and the splash potion splattered all over Harper and her friends.

"Watch it, Theo!" said Morgan.

Morgan was in bad shape. Harper worried that he must be very low on health. "I think we need to retreat so Morgan has a chance to heal."

"YOU GUYS GO," said Theo. "I'll cover you."

"Don't be ridiculous," said Harper. **"IT'S TOO DANGEROUS."**

Just then, thunder rumbled once more and it began to rain. From somewhere nearby, the enderman shrieked as if in pain. Harper whirled around in a circle, but the hostile mob was nowhere to be found.

"They hate the rain," said Morgan. He grimaced. "I don't think it's coming back. We got lucky, and just in time. My hearts are low."

"Drink this," Harper said, and she handed Morgan a healing potion.

"THAT WAS A DISASTER," said Po. "That thing almost handed us our blocky butts."

"We had it under control," said Theo. "It was just an enderman!"

Harper wasn't so sure about either of Theo's points. It hadn't felt like they'd had things under control. **In fact, with Ash gone and Theo here, it felt like their teamwork just wasn't clicking like it had before.**

As for it being "just an enderman" . . . Harper couldn't shake the feeling that there was something different about the mob they'd just fought. It was a little too fast. A little too strong.

And its eyes had glowed red with rage and hate . . . and intelligence. Those eyes would haunt her dreams that night.

Chapter 6

FRAZZLED TEACHERS, MAD SCIENTISTS, UNWANTED APPAREL ... AND THAT'S ALL BEFORE THE END OF LUNCH!

Those red eyes haunted Morgan, too.

Morgan was known throughout Woodsword Middle School as a walking encyclopedia of Minecraft – especially Survival Mode. He knew which mobs could be tamed. He knew the exact elevations to find specific gems. He knew strategies for fighting every hostile mob . . . **and he knew that the enderman they had fought was not normal.**

On their walk to school the next day, he told Jodi all about it. "Endermen are supposed to have purple eyes," he said. "That thing's eyes were red. And I've never heard of any mob being able to

disarm a player like it did Harper. We never did find her sword . . ."

Jodi nodded along as he spoke. She looked lost in thought.

Morgan continued, **"It wasn't like any enderman I've seen.** It was like some kind of . . . Endermonster."

"I'm more worried about the Evoker King," said Jodi. "Did the Endermonster destroy him? And what were those icky mobs we saw in the smoke? There was definitely more than one, right?"

"I'll bet it's Theo's fault," Morgan grumbled.

"Morgan!" said Jodi. "Be nice."

"What? You heard him," said Morgan, waving his arms in the air. **"He's been installing mods behind our backs.** And he was a total mess during the Endermonster fight. It's like he's

never even *heard* of teamwork before!"

Jodi frowned at him. **"Maybe he'd be better at teamwork if you treated him like part of the team."**

"You think it's *my* fault?" Morgan asked. "You can't blame me for his mistakes."

Jodi shook her head. "I'm not blaming you. I'm just pointing out that you aren't always very welcoming to new people. Remember when Ash moved here? You didn't want to include her in anything. But when you started being nice, she became one of your best friends."

"Well, that's the whole problem," said Morgan. **"Theo is no Ash."**

"Just promise me you'll make an effort," said Jodi. "Be a little more welcoming. Please?"

Morgan crossed his arms. "Yeah. Okay. Fine," he said. "I'll make an effort."

Morgan knew he wouldn't have a chance to talk to Theo until lunch. He hoped for an easy, quiet morning in the meantime.

But homeroom got off to a weird start. **"Pop quiz time,"** said Ms Minerva. "Everyone ready?"

The students shared a confused look. Finally, Morgan raised his hand. "Um, Ms Minerva?" he said. "This is homeroom. We don't actually have quizzes or grades in homeroom, right?"

Ms Minerva straightened her glasses. **They were smudged, and her hair was in disarray.** "Oh, yes," she said. "What was I thinking? You're right, Mulligan."

Mulligan? Now Morgan was really worried. "Uh, my name is—"

Morgan was interrupted by the squeal of the loudspeaker coming to life. "Today's morning announcement is as follows," said a voice. **It wasn't the usual robotic voice of the school's announcement AI.** This voice sounded human – but weird. Like someone was

trying to disguise their voice. "The faculty lounge's *exquisite* combo coffee maker and weather prediction device is out of order. Do not expect repairs until *somebody* apologises for insulting it."

Morgan turned to Jodi. **"Is that ... Doc?"** he whispered.

"This concludes the morning announcements," said the voice. "Good luck out there!"

Morgan turned back to get a better look at Ms Minerva. She looked rough. Was this what happened she missed her morning coffee?

"I'm fine!" Ms Minerva said. She rummaged through the lost-and-found box beneath her desk and pulled out a juice box. She squinted at the ingredients. **"Water ... kiwi and pineapple extract (Pineapple? That's weird) ... monodextrosomething concentrate... Why don't they make these things with coffee?"**

"Those two need to make up," Jodi whispered into Morgan's ear.

Morgan agreed. He spent the rest of homeroom

hoping Ms Minerva would hurry to apologise to Doc between classes.

Apparently, there was no apology.

Doc stopped by their table at lunch. **"Greetings, my little Minecrafters!"** she said. "I come to you seeking aid."

Harper perked up, as she always did at the chance to learn from Doc. "What do you need?" she asked. "Is it . . . a science side quest?"

Doc chuckled. "You know me too well. Yes, in fact. I need a few students to take some measurements in the butterfly sanctuary after school."

Po's face drooped. "Aw, I can't," he said glumly. "I have drama club."

"That means we won't be playing Minecraft," said Morgan.

"How come?" said Theo. "We could still play without Po there, right?"

Po gasped theatrically. "Don't you

dare!" he said, outraged by the thought.

"It's an unspoken rule," Jodi explained to Theo. **"If one of us can't make it, we usually don't meet up."**

"You guys have a lot of unspoken rules," Theo said. "Maybe you should write them down."

He chuckled as he said it, so Morgan knew he was trying to make a joke. But it rubbed Morgan the wrong way – like Theo was calling them bossy.

"Anyway," Harper said, glaring at her friends before turning back to Doc, **"I'll help with the measurements."**

"Yeah," Jodi said. "Morgan and I will, too."

"Much appreciated," said Doc. "I would do it myself, you know . . . but Ms Minerva has decided not to give me a ride to my evening badminton match. Which means I have to take my bike. Which means it will be a mad dash to get there in time."

"Gosh," Jodi said. **"That sounds stressful."**

"Oh, I wouldn't want to get a ride in Minerva's car today anyway," said Doc. "Not after I fill it with beetles . . ."

The kids looked shocked.

"Eh-hem . . . I'm just kidding, of course," Doc said as she nervously cleared her throat. "Well, see you in class."

Then she quickly walked away.

"I feel like we're kidding when we call her a mad scientist," said Po. **"But . . . maybe she's actually a mad scientist?"**

"Someone has got to get those two back on the same page," said Jodi. Morgan could see the wheels turning in her head. His sister couldn't stand to see people (or animals) in conflict.

Theo rapped his knuckles on the table to get their attention. "I have a surprise for you all," he said. "I was going to hand these out at the library tonight. But if we're not meeting, I'll give them to you now."

"A surprise?" Morgan echoed. **"I hope it's not a splash potion."** Jodi elbowed him in the ribs.

"I felt bad about how things went yesterday," Theo continued. "So I stayed up late to make these."

Theo pulled a T-shirt from a beat-up old

cardboard box. It was bright green, and quite large, and in big, blocky letters it said **BLOCK HEADZ.**

"There's one for everybody!" he said, and he passed out the T-shirts.

"Interesting colour," said Po. **"Sort of a . . . booger green."**

"I don't understand the 'Z' at all," said Harper.

"What's a blockhead?" asked Jodi.

"We are!" said Theo. **"I figured we should have a team name. So . . . Block Headz."**

"That's so nice, Theo," said Jodi, and she elbowed Morgan again. "Don't you think so, big brother?"

Morgan held up his T-shirt. It was all wrong. He understood that Theo was trying to be nice, but . . . he just hated the shirt. *Hated it!*

"It's a nice gesture, man," said Po.

"I'll be sure to wear it soon," said Harper.

"Maybe I'll get matching . . . um . . . nail polish!" said Jodi.

Morgan realised he had been silent for a long time. Everyone was looking at him.

"It's . . . cool," he said. **"Thanks, Theo."**

But he didn't sound very convincing. He could

tell by the disappointed look on Theo's face.

Just then, the bell rang. Lunch was over, and everyone started packing up their things.

"Saved by the bell," Morgan muttered under his breath.

Jodi gave him a dirty look. But what could he do? **Morgan didn't want to be mean, but from his perspective, Theo made it hard to be nice.**

Chapter 7

"METAMORPHOSIS" IS A BIG WORD THAT MEANS "CHANGE". LET'S JUST HOPE IT'S FOR THE BETTER . . .

After school, Jodi made her way to the butterfly sanctuary, previously known as the computer lab.

When she opened the door, she was pleasantly surprised to see a familiar face.

"**Baron Sweetcheeks!**" she said. "What are you doing here?"

The class hamster squeaked as if to say hello. He had been put into a plastic hamster ball, and he rolled right up to Jodi. She picked him up, ball and all.

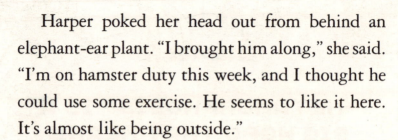

Harper poked her head out from behind an elephant-ear plant. "I brought him along," she said. "I'm on hamster duty this week, and I thought he could use some exercise. He seems to like it here. It's almost like being outside."

"Yeah, what happened to the air-conditioning?" Morgan pulled at his sweaty shirt. "It's sweltering in here. **like it's an actual jungle!**"

"That's on purpose," said Harper. "Doc was keeping all the caterpillars in a terrarium so she could control the temperature and humidity levels for them. But now . . . since they escaped . . ."

"This whole room is the terrarium," said Morgan. "Got it."

"We just have to take some measurements," said Harper. "We'll report back to Doc, and she'll figure out if she needs to bring in more plants or adjust the thermostat or anything like that."

"I hope these little guys appreciate all this," said Morgan, squinting to get a good look at a cocoon.

"I'm sure they do!" said Jodi. "When they hatch, they'll know we took good care of them. Like the baron here." She placed the hamster

ball back on the ground, and Baron Sweetcheeks resumed rolling around the room.

"It's weird, though," said Morgan. **"These things were caterpillars less than a week ago.** And they're going to be butterflies?"

"That's right," said Harper. "They're going through *metamorphosis* – which is a fancy word for 'change.'"

Morgan frowned. "I feel like we're all going through metamorphosis. Nothing is the same as it was before."

Jodi patted her brother on the back. "Nothing is ever the same as before," she said. **"Change is constant."** She looked over her shoulder. "I just wish we would sprout wings. That's a change I could really enjoy!"

Just then, **Harper's backpack chimed.**

"Ooh!" Harper said. "That's my phone." She rummaged around in a pocket. Then she pulled out the phone she had once upgraded with some of Doc's old equipment – to strange results. "It's a video call," Harper said with a grin. "From our old friend—"

"**Ash!**" cried Jodi. She squeezed in close to Harper so that she could get a better look. "How are you? I like your hair! What's the weather like over there?"

"Hi, Jodi," said Ash. "Everything's good here, but I miss you guys."

"We miss you, too," said Morgan. He squeezed in on Harper's other side.

Baron Sweetcheeks squeaked at the sound of Ash's voice, and Harper laughed. "Baron Sweetcheeks says hi. Either that or he's asking for dinner."

"Baron Sweetcheeks is the best," said Ash. "**My new class pet is a snake,** you guys. A snake! It gives me the creeps."

Baron Sweetcheeks squeaked in agreement.

"Aw, snakes are all right," said Jodi. She wouldn't mind having a snake, if only she could find one that didn't eat cute little rodents. Were there vegetarian snakes? She made a note to look that up next time they were in the library.

"**Are we playing Minecraft tonight?**" asked Ash. "I'm finally free!"

"Bad timing," Harper said glumly. "We're helping Doc with a project. And Po's got a club meeting."

"Aw, too bad," said Ash. "I keep missing you guys. But we'll find time soon, I'm sure."

"I hope so," Morgan said. "It's not the same without you. Theo is *super* annoying."

"**Yikes,**" said Ash. "That's pretty harsh, Morgan."

"It's the truth!" he said. "I don't understand his jokes. He's a terrible team player – he just always acts like he's in charge, and then he gets in the way. **He likes to tell us he's some sort of coding genius, but I'm beginning to think he couldn't hack his way out of a paper bag.**"

"Ouch," said a voice. Jodi's heart sank immediately. She knew whose voice that was.

They turned to see Theo standing in the doorway. He was holding a pizza box and wearing his Block Headz shirt. And he looked utterly, completely heartbroken. "I was just . . . I thought you guys might want some pineapple pizza, but . . ."

He couldn't finish the sentence. He spun around and bolted into the hallway.

"Theo, wait!" said Jodi. She hurried after him, but she had to step around plants and a hyperactive hamster in a ball. By the time she got to the door, **Theo was gone.**

Morgan face-palmed. "That wasn't great," he said.

"No, it wasn't," Jodi said crossly. "I was already worried about Doc and Ms Minerva fighting. Now I have to worry about you two. What did I tell you about being nice?"

"I didn't know he was there. I'll make it up to him," said Morgan. "Somehow." His face was red. *At least he has the good sense to be embarrassed,* Jodi thought. *That's a start.*

"It sounds like there's a lot happening over there," Ash said through the phone. "Do you guys want to fill me in?"

Morgan, Jodi and Harper all sighed at the same time.

"It's a long story," said Harper.

"I've got time," said Ash. "Tell me all about it."

Jodi smiled and picked up Baron Sweetcheeks in his hamster ball. Ash always made her feel better. **And Ash always made their problems feel solvable.**

It was nice to know that the distance between them didn't change that.

Chapter 8

LET'S BE HONEST: PINEAPPLE ON PIZZA IS JUST WEIRD, EVEN IF IT PROVIDES A BALANCE BETWEEN SWEET AND SAVOURY.

Theo felt a terrible mix of emotions in his belly. He was angry at Morgan for the things he'd said. He was worried that all his friends might feel the same way Morgan did. Worst of all, he felt guilty.

Because what if Morgan was right? What if Theo's mods had broken the game somehow? **What if the Evoker King had been destroyed . . . and it was all his fault?**

After Theo stormed out of the butterfly sanctuary, he didn't stop moving until he'd made it across the street to Stonesword. He didn't even realise he was still holding the pizza box until

Mr Malory pointed it out to him.

"Sorry, Theo," he said. "No food allowed."

"Oh," Theo said, looking at the box in his hands. "Do you want it, sir? I'm not really hungry anymore. **It's pineapple...**"

Mr Malory grimaced as he took the pizza box. "Not my favourite. But I'll put it in the break room. The volunteers from the high school will eat anything." He looked towards the door, as if expecting other students to file in behind Theo. **"Where's the rest of the group?** I thought you all travelled together."

"Sometimes," Theo said, looking a little embarrassed. "But other times, they treat me like

I'm not really part of the group. I don't get it. I try so hard to fit in . . ."

Mr Malory nodded. "I've been there. We've *all* been there," he said. "But sometimes, trying to fit in is the wrong thing to do. **Because if you try too hard, you're not being yourself. And your friends should like you for who you are.**"

For a moment, Theo was silent, his jaw working like he was chewing a piece of sticky caramel.

"Thanks, Mr Malory," he said, a smile slowly returning to his face. "You've given me something to think about. **Are the computers free?**"

"They are today," he said. "But eventually, other kids are going to find them. I might have to limit screen time . . ."

Theo's smile dropped again. "Really?" he said.

Mr Malory chuckled. "You go right ahead and enjoy yourself. Forget about your problems for a while."

"Okay," said Theo. But he didn't intend to forget about his problems. **He intended to fix them.**

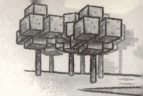

Because Mr Malory had told him to be himself. **And who he was . . . was a problem-solver.**

Even when that meant breaking the rules.

Theo had played Minecraft by himself plenty of times. But he still wasn't used to being alone in the strange VR goggle version of Minecraft. The silence made him feel nervous.

Of course, he probably *should* be nervous, he thought. **The Endermonster was out there somewhere.**

And Theo meant to find it.

Theo raided one of the Shack's many storage chests. He selected a set of diamond armour, a diamond sword and some healing potions. He felt a lot safer now . . . **but he would have to be sure to put everything back,** or Morgan would be even more annoyed with him.

He crept carefully through the forest, retracing their path from the day before. In the clearing

where they'd battled, **the footprints made a big, messy jumble of squares.** But Theo picked up the Endermonster's tracks just outside the clearing.

The mob's trail led him out of the forest, across a sunflower plain and right to the foot of a low mountain. The footprints disappeared occasionally, and Theo was forced to wander around until he found where they picked up again. There was only one explanation for the gaps in the trail: **the mob was teleporting as it travelled.** It never teleported very far, but still, Theo was losing precious time. The sun had set, and darkness had fallen on the Overworld. Using a torch to see more clearly, Theo picked up the Endermonster's trail once more.

Even in his diamond armour, Theo felt a shiver of fear.

It was when the night felt its darkest that he found the Endermonster. **He saw its eyes first.** Those frightening red eyes seemed to glow in the dark.

Then Theo realised his mistake. If he could see those eyes . . .

. . . those eyes could see him, too!

The Endermonster emitted a terrible scream. The sound chilled Theo to the core. He lifted his sword to defend himself—

But it was teleported right out of his hands!

Okay, thought Theo. *That's fine. I didn't want to hurt him anyway. I just wanted to get a good look at him.*

That goal would be easier to achieve now – since the Endermonster had teleported right into Theo's face!

Theo took a quick step backward, barely avoiding the hostile mob's swinging fist. He forced himself to stay calm. He had a theory about what the mob *really* was . . . but he needed proof. He needed some sign that this wasn't an enderman at all, that it was actually—

POW! The Endermonster's second swing connected. Theo almost fell over.

This mob hit *hard.* But at least Theo had powerful armour to protect him.

The Endermonster emitted a low howl. **Its eyes flashed bright red.** And Theo's diamond chest plate . . . disappeared.

The Endermonster had teleported his armour right off him!

Now Theo worried he was really in trouble. Maybe he shouldn't have tried to do this by

himself. Maybe everything Morgan had said about him was true.

Theo backed up against a tree. The Endermonster stepped closer. It loomed above him. Theo searched its face for any sign of intelligence or compassion. **"PLEASE,"** he said.

Something strange happened then. The Endermonster opened its mouth, as if ready to howl again.

This time, it spoke words.

"DON'T LOOK AT ME!"

Theo gasped. The Endermonster had spoken . . . with the Evoker King's voice.

Theo realised that his theory was correct. The

Evoker King's code hadn't been destroyed. It had been changed.

Changed . . . into *this*.

He tried to take comfort in that knowledge as the Endermonster raised its arms to strike him down.

Suddenly, a flask flew through the air. It struck the Endermonster square in the back. The mob's eyes went wide with surprise **– and then it teleported away in the blink of an eye.**

With the Endermonster no longer right in front of

him, Theo saw that someone else had followed its trail. Someone very unexpected — but a welcome surprise.

"ASH?!" said Theo.

"Are you all right, Theo?" she asked.

"I am now." He rubbed his aching head. "Your timing was perfect. What did you hit that mob with?"

"Just water," she answered. "Morgan and Harper filled me in. **I KNOW THAT THING ISN'T A NORMAL MOB . . .** but it seems to hate water just as much as any other enderman."

"I should have thought of that," Theo said, scolding himself. **"MY WEAPON SURE DIDN'T HELP. AND NOW I'VE LOST OUR ONLY DIAMOND SWORD."**

"You mean this diamond sword?" Ash held it up for Theo to see. "I found it under a tree nearby. **I WAS WONDERING WHERE IT CAME FROM."**

Theo smiled slightly. "That's a relief. Now Morgan will just yell at me a little, instead of yelling at me a lot."

Ash chuckled. "I might know a thing or two about that," she said. "Remember, it wasn't so long ago that I was the new kid." She handed him the

sword. **"LET'S GET OUT OF HERE BEFORE THAT THING COMES BACK.** Then you can tell me what you're doing here alone . . . and maybe I can give you some advice for dealing with Morgan."

Theo smiled a real smile this time. "That would be great."

As they walked back to the Shack, they kept their eyes open. They didn't see the missing diamond armour. But they didn't see any red eyes beneath the trees, either. So Theo considered himself lucky.

"Here's the thing about Morgan," said Ash. "He is the kindest, most loyal friend a person can have. **BUT HE'S VERY PICKY ABOUT WHO HE CONSIDERS A FRIEND."**

"I definitely got that impression," said Theo. "I know he thinks I'm bad at teamwork."

"TEAMWORK IS SKILL. It's like . . . playing the piano," said Ash. "Anyone can do it. But it takes constant practice to do it well. Even Morgan has to practice it. He likes being in charge. But sometimes he needs to be reminded that he's not the boss of Minecraft." Ash chuckled. "I got very good at reminding him of that."

"So where do I start?" asked Theo. "I don't think I can go into school tomorrow and say, **'HEY, MORGAN, PLEASE STOP BEING BOSSY.'**"

"No, that won't help," said Ash. "You need to show him that you care about the team. You need to show him he can *trust* you. That means being honest . . . including telling the truth about what you're up to in here."

Theo thought about that. **He still hadn't been honest about all his modding.**

"What if the truth just makes him angrier?"

Ash thought about that for a moment. "It might. But you can't let fear get in the way of being honest. Not if you want a *real* friendship with Morgan and the others."

Theo sighed. It sounded so simple when Ash said it. But he knew she was right.

As they approached the Shack, Theo caught a glimpse of something out of the corner of his eye. **A glimmer of light shone in the sky.**

At first he thought the Endermonster had found them. But it was something else . . .

"Hey, Ash," said Theo. "Do you see that?"

Ash squinted. "That's definitely weird," she agreed. "Let's climb that hill and get a better look."

They got closer to the anomaly, but it was hard to see. It was like a patch of deeper black in the darkness. But its edges glimmered like an oil slick.

It was a hole. **A tear in the sky.**

Theo had never seen anything like it. Neither had Ash.

"SOMETHING ELSE TO WORRY ABOUT," said Theo.

"One thing at a time," said Ash. "You've got a big conversation with Morgan and the others tomorrow. Focus on that for now."

"Right," Theo said. **That conversation - his confession - felt more terrifying than some random glitch in the Minecraft sky.**

And he wasn't looking forward to it. Not at all.

Chapter 9

A REVELATION!
A EUREKA MOMENT!
A CHANGE OF HEART!
ALL LIKE BUTTERFLIES
TAKING FLIGHT!

Po was eating a peanut butter sandwich for lunch when Jodi and Harper presented their plan for saving their teachers' friendship. Morgan nodded along as he took a bite of banana. Theo sat listening in silence.

"We have to do *something*," said Jodi. **"We can't just sit by while their friendship ends over some cocoons and a cybernetic coffee pot."**

"But what can we do?" Po asked.

"We've already started," Jodi answered. "After we finished in the butterfly sanctuary yesterday, I removed the beetles from Ms Minerva's car. Doc was *not* joking."

"And I got permission to go to the faculty lounge this morning," said Harper. **"I was able to get the coffee machine up and running."**

"I thought Ms Minerva seemed better this morning," said Morgan. "She got my name right during attendance, anyway."

"You're a genius, Harper," Po said. "How did you fix the high-tech coffee machine so quickly?"

Harper grinned. "It wasn't broken. Doc had just unplugged it, and nobody had thought to check the power cord."

"Mad science," said Po. "I'm telling you! Right, Theo?"

Theo didn't say anything. In fact, he had hardly said anything all morning. **His mind was clearly elsewhere.**

"Here's what we do next," said Jodi. "We're going to ask the yearbook club for photos – lots of photos. *Years* of photos. Everything they have of Doc and Ms Minerva."

"We'll make a photo album," said Harper. "And then we'll scan it. I'll upload a digital version of the album to Doc's tablet while the rest of you sneak the physical album into the library. You can shelve it next to the young adult vampire novels, where Ms Minerva will definitely find it eventually."

"She does love those vampire novels," Po said.

"And there you have it!" Jodi said. "Violins swell, they realise their friendship is precious and we have saved the day."

"It's brilliant," said Po. And he took a big bite of his sandwich.

Theo chose that moment to finally speak. **"I have to tell you all something,"** he said. **"I made a mistake."**

Po tried to ask, "What do you mean?" But with his mouth full of peanut butter and bread, it sounded more like, "Waddle a meme?" Everyone gave him a weird look. But Theo answered his question anyway.

"I've been modding," he said. "You all saw the footprint mod. But that's just the tip of the iceberg. I've been making all kinds of stuff. And . . ." He took a deep breath. "I've even been messing with some of Doc's mods."

"I knew it!" Morgan growled, and the others all shushed him.

"Go on, Theo," said Harper.

"I didn't mean to cause problems," Theo continued. "But the best way to learn coding is by playing with somebody else's code. I thought if I figured out what Doc had done to the game . . . if I could wrap my head

around all her modding . . . then I could figure out what went wrong with the Evoker King. I thought it would help me fix him."

Jodi pressed her palms to her cheeks. "Theo," she said. **"Did . . . did your modding . . . did it destroy the Evoker King?"**

"No. Maybe." Theo said. "I don't know. But the Evoker King isn't gone. He's just . . . different."

"What do you mean?" asked Harper. "Different how?"

"The Evoker King didn't explode. He transformed," Theo said. **"He transformed . . . into the Endermonster."**

Po gasped. He was lucky he didn't choke on his sandwich.

"That creepy thing is . . . was . . . our friend?" Jodi asked.

"Poor Bob," said Po.

"Is it permanent?" Harper asked. **"Can we fix it?"**

"I . . . I don't know," said Theo. "I think so. I'll do whatever it takes to try."

Po noticed Morgan wasn't saying anything.

Theo was afraid to even look in his direction.

Before anybody could say anything else, **the cafe doors burst open.** Doc hurried over to their table. "Sanctuary volunteers!" she cried. **"The cocoons are hatching! Come quick!"**

Doc didn't wait for them to respond. She was running out the door before Po had even processed what she had said.

"Let's go!" said Jodi.

"We're not done discussing this," Morgan said.

Harper was already out of her seat. "We can talk in the sanctuary. Come on," she said, tugging on Theo. "I am *not* missing this!"

Po trembled with anticipation. **A few of the butterflies had already emerged,** but most of the cocoons were just beginning to hatch. He marvelled at the sight. Each new butterfly stepped lightly out of its shell, as if uncertain or shy. But then it slowly spread its wings and gave them a test flap or two. Some instinct told it how to use those wings, and it quickly took flight.

He had thought they would all look the same. But each butterfly was a different colour. Blue, orange, pink, green. **It was like being inside a living prism.**

A butterfly with light-blue wings landed on Po's nose. It tickled, and when he laughed, the startled insect flew away.

"It's kind of amazing," he said. "They grew wings while inside their cocoons. They just grew a whole new body part!"

"And not just the wings," said Harper. "They also develop longer legs and antennae and more complex eyes. Metamorphosis is complicated — they need those cocoons to keep them safe while they're going through all those changes." She frowned. "It's weird. **I actually thought I saw a butterfly in the game recently.** Right after the Evoker King split open."

"Me too!" said Po. "I saw a bunch of them through the smoke."

Theo went pale. "That's strange," he said.

"A butterfly was one of the mods I made. I was inspired to do it because I knew we'd be learning about them in Doc's class."

"So you made digital butterflies," Morgan said, "and now they're loose in the game?"

Theo shook his head. "That's not possible. After I made sure that mod worked, I uninstalled it. **The code for butterflies exists now, but it isn't active.**"

Po saw Jodi's eyes light up. "It's almost like . . . like someone is trying to tell us something."

Harper gave Jodi a long look. "What do you mean?"

"Think about it," Jodi said. "According to Theo, the Evoker King just went through a major transformation. **A metamorphosis!** And then, as soon as that happened, butterflies appeared in the game."

"So you think the Evoker King was trying to tell us what had happened?" Po said. "By using Theo's butterfly code?"

Jodi nodded enthusiastically. "Yeah! I mean, we kept saying he was 'solid stone.' *Petrified.* But what if the stone was more like a protective shell? A *cocoon,* keeping him safe while he changed?"

"It sort of makes sense," Harper said. "He wasn't programmed to be our friend. He *decided* to do that. And he was learning emotions and how to deal with them. His program was changing, and rapidly. **What if he spun a cocoon to protect himself while his code rewrote itself into a new and improved Evoker King?"**

"But that would mean . . ." Theo grinned. "That would mean it isn't my fault that he changed! He was changing anyway."

Harper frowned. "We don't know anything for sure. But I don't think he would have become the Endermonster. I think his programming was in flux . . . it was *vulnerable* . . ."

"And when I messed with Doc's code, **I created a monster.**" Theo hung his head.

The door to the sanctuary opened. Po wasn't surprised to see Doc enter. But he was surprised to see Ms Minerva following right behind her, holding Baron Sweetcheeks in her hands.

"You see, Minerva?" said Doc. "It's just like I said!"

"What a marvel," said Ms Minerva. **"I never imagined I'd witness something like this."**

The two teachers — and the hamster — shared a smile.

Po whispered to Jodi, "I guess they aren't fighting anymore?"

Jodi whispered, **"I'm still making that photo album just in case."**

Morgan looked at the teachers oohing and aahing at each new butterfly. Then he looked at Theo, who seemed miserable with guilt.

Morgan must have been inspired by the sight of the teachers putting their grudge aside. **He put a hand on Theo's shoulder** and said, **"It's not your fault."**

Po hadn't expected that.

"You were trying to help," Morgan continued. "We all understand. And now that you've been honest with us . . . **we can fix it somehow."**

"You mean it?" asked Theo.

"That's what teams are for," said Harper, and she put a hand on Theo's other shoulder. "We share

the problem. We solve it together."

"Where do we start?" asked Jodi.

"Well, first, we should probably make sure the Endermonster doesn't wander off," said Theo. "If it does, we might never find it again."

"So we need to capture it?" said Po. "That sounds hard, considering we can't even look at it."

"Well, I do know one trick we can use," said Morgan. **"It's a way to look at an enderman**

without angering it. It should work on the Endermonster, too."

"Okay, so with Morgan's trick, we can look directly at the scary mob," said Po. "Next problem: How do you capture something that can just teleport away?"

"I had an idea about that, actually," said Harper. "What if we use its power against it? **What if it teleports ... right into a trap?**"

"I like that," Po said, and he felt a little thrill at the idea.

Time to show the Endermonster that it had messed with the wrong team.

Chapter 10

PUMPKINS! THEY'RE WHAT ALL THE MONSTER HUNTERS ARE WEARING THIS SEASON.

Harper had changed her skin to an outfit better suited for capturing a hostile mob. She figured if Po could change his skin for every new adventure and whim, she could change hers for more practical reasons. But at the moment, she felt ridiculous. "Morgan, **TELL ME AGAIN WHY I HAVE TO WEAR THIS PUMPKIN ON MY HEAD,**" she demanded.

"It's safer this way. I promise!" Morgan told her. "The Endermonster has powers that an enderman doesn't have. But it still acts like an enderman." **He put a pumpkin**

on his own head. "And an enderman attacks anyone who looks at it . . . unless that person is wearing a pumpkin."

"Personally, I am a big fan of this plan," said Po. "I could really *lose my head* over how cool it is!" In addition to the pumpkin head, **he was wearing all black clothes, with a dark cape hanging from his shoulders.** He looked like the Headless Horseman in "The Legend of Sleepy Hollow."

Harper sighed. She couldn't shake the feeling that Morgan was playing a prank on them. But she knew he wouldn't be so silly when they were on such an important mission.

They had to capture this mob or whatever it was if they had any hope of saving their digital friend.

"Let's review the plan," Harper said. "We need to dig a pit and then line the pit with soul sand, which I picked up last time we were in the Nether."

"Because according to Morgan, endermen can't teleport when they're standing on soul sand," said Jodi.

"That trick only works during the day," said Morgan. **"So we have to time this just right."**

"So we'll get the Endermonster to teleport into the pit," said Po. "It won't be able to teleport out of the pit, and it will be too deep to climb out."

"That just leaves the question of bait," said Theo. "What do we use to lure the Endermonster into the pit?"

"Not what," said Morgan. *"Who."* He turned his pumpkin-head gaze to Theo. "How serious were you when you said you'd do anything to fix this?"

Harper knew that it wasn't really possible, but she thought Theo's avatar looked a little queasy.

The Endermonster was easy to find. It still hadn't travelled very far from the site of their first battle. **The mob shuffled from tree to tree,** moving blocks around seemingly at random. Harper passed out flasks of an electric-blue liquid. "Everybody drink up," she said.

"It looks like a sports drink," said Po.

Harper grinned. "You're sort of right. These are potions of swiftness. **WE NEED TO BE QUICK AGAINST AN ENEMY WHO CAN TELEPORT.**"

Theo drank his potion down. "I feel faster already," said Theo. "Wish me luck."

"We've got your back," Jodi promised.

Theo removed the pumpkin from his head. He looked right at the Endermonster.

"PEEK-A-BOO!" he cried. "I see you, Endermonster!"

The Endermonster whirled at the sound of Theo's voice. It emitted a bloodcurdling shriek.

"Now, Theo," said Harper. "Go. Run!"

Theo turned and ran, hoping he would be fast enough. At the same moment, the Endermonster teleported to where Theo had just been standing, slamming its fists down on empty grass.

The mob shrieked in frustration. It scanned the

forest with its sinister red eyes. When it spotted Theo, it teleported again. Once again, it just missed him.

"THEO'S STAYING AHEAD OF IT, THANKS TO THE SWIFTNESS POTION!" said Harper.

"And we need to keep up with them so we can help if his luck — or his speed — runs out," said Morgan. "Come on, everybody!"

They all ran, weaving around the trees of the forest. **Theo was in the lead, screaming his head off.** The Endermonster was right at his heels. And Harper and her friends followed in the Endermonster's wake, their pumpkins protecting them from its anger.

Finally, they reached the end of the forest and the edge of the pit. Theo didn't even slow down. He leapt right into the hole. **He would probably take some fall damage.** Still, that would hurt less than a direct punch from the creature pursuing him.

But would it follow? Harper held her breath.

Then she let out a whoop of triumph. **The**

Endermonster took the bait — it teleported itself right into the pit.

Theo dodged one more swing of its arms. Then he leapt for a ladder on the pit's far side. He quickly climbed out of reach of the creature's long limbs, and as soon as he was back on the grass, Morgan was there, smashing the ladder to bits with a pickaxe.

They'd done it. Their plan had worked. **They'd captured the Endermonster!**

But now that they had it . . . what would they do with it?

Ash found her friends near the Shack. They stood at the edge of a great pit, and they looked very serious.

But their eyes lit up with joy when they saw her.

"ASH!" cried Jodi, and **she flung herself into Ash's blocky arms.**

"Hey, Jodi," said Ash. "Good to see you, too. But, um . . . why is Po wearing a pumpkin on his head?"

"Fashion!" said Po. He threw his arms around both Jodi and Ash, and then Harper and Morgan joined in, **making for an epic group hug.** Theo kept his distance, though. Shyly, he waved hello from the edge of the pit.

"We caught it, Ash," said Theo. "We have the Endermonster trapped."

"For now," said Morgan. He looked at the sun, already lowering in the sky. "When the sun sets, the mob will be able to teleport again. And we might not get a second chance."

"So what do we do now?" asked Harper. **"WE NEED MORE TIME TO FIGURE OUT HOW TO FIX THE EVOKER KING."**

"Could we make a cage?" Po asked. "Some kind of box the Endermonster can't teleport out of?"

"Maybe we need to strike it down," said Morgan. "If we got its health down, it might respawn in its original form." He pulled out a bow. "From up here, it would be like shooting fish in a barrel."

"That is *risky,* big brother," said Jodi. "And kind of mean."

"Letting him run free is risky, too," said Morgan.

Ash looked down at the mob. It paced on the soul sand. It seemed anxious, even scared. It looked up at her, and its red eyes met hers.

It shrieked. It shook. It tried to teleport . . . But it was stuck.

"Don't look at me!" it cried. "Don't look at me! STOP LOOKING AT ME!"

Ash took a step back. It was too strange, hearing

the Evoker King's voice coming from the monster.

"It sounds angry," said Po.

"Not angry," Ash said. "Terrified." She turned to Morgan. **"PUT THE WEAPON AWAY,** Morgan. Attacking it doesn't seem right."

Morgan put the bow back in his inventory. But he still had a hard look in his eyes. "What else can we do?" he asked.

Ash put her fists on her hips. **"HAS ANYONE TRIED TALKING TO IT?"**

"Talking?" said Po. "To Creepy McGlowyEyes down there?"

"It can speak with the Evoker King's voice," Ash replied. "Does that mean it can listen with the Evoker King's ears?"

Everyone was silent for a moment.

"I'll try it," said Theo.

Then he thought about what he'd just said. "But only if the group agrees," he added. "From now on, **I WON'T MAKE DECISIONS THAT AFFECT ALL OF US** unless I discuss things with the team first."

"What exactly are you offering to do?" asked Morgan, raising a rectangular eyebrow..

"I want to go back down into the pit," Theo answered. "I want to talk to the Endermonster. **JUST ME. ALL ALONE.**"

Chapter 11

THE ENDERMONSTER IS WHAT? YOU'RE PULLING MY STONE LEG!

Theo didn't put the pumpkin back on his head. He wanted the Endermonster to really *see* him. **Maybe the part of it that was once the Evoker King would recognise Theo as a friend.**

He would just have to avoid making eye contact. He wanted to be very careful not to anger it again, now that the mob had finally calmed down.

He could feel his friends' eyes on him as he descended the ladder into the pit. They were nervous. Morgan, especially. **Because Morgan didn't like it when things were out of his control.**

And this time, it all came down to Theo.

Once he was off the ladder, Theo kept his eyes on the ground. The soul sand was eerie. As if this situation weren't frightening enough!

"I, uh, I come in peace," he said. **"I JUST WANT TO TALK."**

The Endermonster didn't say anything. But it didn't attack, either.

"Do you remember me? I'm Theo. We were both going to be 'the new kid' at the same time."

He took a shuffling step forward. **"YOU CALLED YOURSELF THE EVOKER KING."**

The mob made that horrible shrieking sound. Theo flinched, and he held his hands up in front of him. But he kept his eyes on the ground.

The shriek faded. **And the Endermonster spoke.**

"Not Evoker King," it said. "Evoker King's . . . **FEAR."**

"Fear?" Theo felt it himself. "I don't understand."

"Evoker King . . . **WAS ONE.** Evoker King . . . **IS SIX.**"

It took Theo a moment to make sense of what the Endermonster was saying. He gasped as the truth sank in.

Did he understand correctly? **Was such a bizarre metamorphosis possible?**

The Evoker King hadn't just become this new mob. He had become *six* new mobs.

Theo remembered the moment when Jodi had convinced the Evoker King to be their friend. The

Evoker King had been scared. **He was terrified of change.**

Was the Endermonster that piece of him? The part of him that was afraid?

"Listen to me," Theo said. "I know what it's like . . . to be afraid. I know what it's like to not want people to see you. Because what if they don't like what they see?" He took a deep, shaky breath. "It feels safer to be invisible. **SAFER . . . BUT IT'S SO LONELY.** Aren't you lonely?"

The Endermonster didn't say anything. But Theo could hear it making the strange,

otherworldly sounds of an enderman. It was close.
He took another small step forward.

"I'm going to look at you now," he said. "I know it's scary. But I want you to be brave. Because I'm your *friend.* And you have to let your friends see the real you."

Theo raised his square chin. He gazed into the Endermonster's face. **He looked right into its blood-red eyes.**

"Not afraid," it said.

"Good," said Theo. "That's good."

The mob's eyes glowed red. Its whole body glowed. It leaned forward and whispered something in Theo's ear.

Theo didn't have a chance to respond. The Endermonster was engulfed in a burst of light — **light in the shape of blocky, pixelated butterflies.** There was a swarm of them, and they washed over Theo, filling his vision with colour. He had to shield his eyes and look away.

When the butterflies had all faded or flown away, **Theo saw that the Endermonster was gone.** Where it had stood just a moment before, there was now a long, rectangular block.

"What *is* that?" asked Jodi.

"It's a leg," said Theo. **"IT'S THE FIRST PIECE OF THE EVOKER KING."**

"The first piece?" said Ash.

"You mean . . . that was just the beginning?" Morgan asked.

"I'll explain everything," said Theo. **He poked the leg.** "But first, we need to figure out who's putting that leg in their inventory."

Chapter 12

ASIDE FROM THE STRANDS OF TWISTED CODE AND AN OMINOUS WARNING OF IMPENDING DOOM, THIS IS A TOTALLY HAPPY ENDING!

With Doc's permission, **THEO RETURNED TO STONESWORD LIBRARY DURING HIS LUNCH PERIOD** the next day. He had promised to uninstall his mods – at least until the team had a chance to vote on which ones would be helpful.

That part was easy. But when Theo saw Doc's code, he gasped.

Lines of code were missing. **Files had been deleted.** The mod code that made their Minecraft game so special . . . was no longer complete.

Theo didn't know enough about programming to know exactly what this meant. But he knew enough to realise that it would be trouble.

Clearly, it wasn't just the Evoker King who had changed. **THE GAME ITSELF HAD CHANGED.**

On his way out of the library, Theo saw Ms Minerva, Doc and Mr Malory taking a lunch break together. **They were sitting by the Stonesword statue.** They were all smiling and laughing.

Mr Malory spotted him first. "Hey, Theo," he said. "Did you solve that problem you were having with your friends?"

"I think so," Theo said. "I took your advice to be myself, and I took my friend Ash's advice to be honest, and I sort of mashed both pieces of advice together." He shrugged. **"I want my friends to see and accept the real me.** I think it's going to be fine."

Ms Minerva nodded. "Wise words, Theo," she said. "Just remember – friendship takes work. And that work is never really done."

"*Some* friendships take more work than others," Doc said, and she cackled when Ms Minerva gave her a look.

"I don't get it," Theo said. "I mean . . . I don't want to be rude . . . but two days ago, **I thought you two hated each other."**

Doc clucked her tongue. "We could never hate each other. We've been friends too long for that."

"Sometimes friends disagree," added Ms Minerva. "Sometimes they disagree *strongly*. And that's okay. As long as you respect each other and can agree on the big things."

"The big things?" Theo echoed.

"Sure," said the teacher. "For instance, Doc and

I both believe in the importance of education. **We agree that there's real joy to be found as a teacher.** And we think you kids deserve the very best."

"And we agree that the butterfly sanctuary is a wonderful addition to the school," Doc added. "Especially if it gives me the chance to update some of our systems. **Woodsword is going to be truly cutting-edge before I'm done!"**

Ms Minerva threw up her hands in surrender. "Sometimes a little chaos is all right, I suppose."

"Oh!" said Mr Malory. "That reminds me." **He plucked the VR headset from Theo's hands.** "We can't have these things floating around. We need to get them checked into the system."

"But . . . ," said Theo. "But we've been taking those home at night. To keep them safe."

"They're perfectly safe here, Theo," said Mr Malory. "What could go wrong in a media centre?"

Mr Malory smiled, but that didn't make Theo feel any better. **And it was clear that**

Theo would have to leave the goggles behind . . . where just about *anybody* could use them.

Maybe moving the computer lab to Stonesword wasn't going to be such a good thing after all.

Another problem for later, Theo thought. Those seemed to be stacking up lately. **Like a tower of blocks that was bound to come crashing down.**

Theo crossed the crossing, stepping back onto school grounds . . . and right into a very welcome surprise.

A very welcome, very green surprise.

"We're still not calling ourselves the Block Headz," said Morgan. **"But I admit the shirts are kind of fun."** Morgan, Harper, Po and Jodi were all in a row, wearing their T-shirts with pride. And Harper was holding a pizza box.

"We figured we owed you a pizza," she said.

"We even got pineapple."

"On *half* of it," said Po. **"It's a weird topping, man."**

"Call it a compromise!" Jodi said. She held up Harper's phone. "Right, Ash?"

"That's right," Ash said through the phone. "Welcome to the team, Theo! For real this time."

"And . . . ?" said Jodi, and she gave her brother a look.

"I am sorry for making you feel unwelcome — you're not as annoying as I said you were," Morgan mumbled. Then he grinned. "As Ash and Jodi have reminded me, I can be a little intense."

Theo smiled. "It's all right. I can be intense, too, in my own way." He rubbed the back of his head. "I made a lot of decisions without checking with you guys first. **I kept secrets. I did it because I was afraid to make you mad."** He shrugged. "I've never had a close group of friends like this.

It's taking me some time to get used to it."

"We'll work it out," said Morgan. "We're good at solving problems. **Although I still don't understand how my diamond armour ended up in a tree…"**

Theo kept his lips sealed about that. And on the phone Ash smirked, keeping mum as well.

"Then it's settled," Ash said happily, changing

the subject. "Now, if only I could figure out how to eat pizza through the phone, this would be a totally happy ending!"

Everybody laughed at that. Theo felt his worries float away on the sound of their happiness.

Most of his worries. He couldn't forget what he had seen in the mod code, and he couldn't forget the Endermonster's final whispered words of warning.

"Beware," it had said. **"THE FAULT . . . WILL DESTROY THE OVERWORLD."**

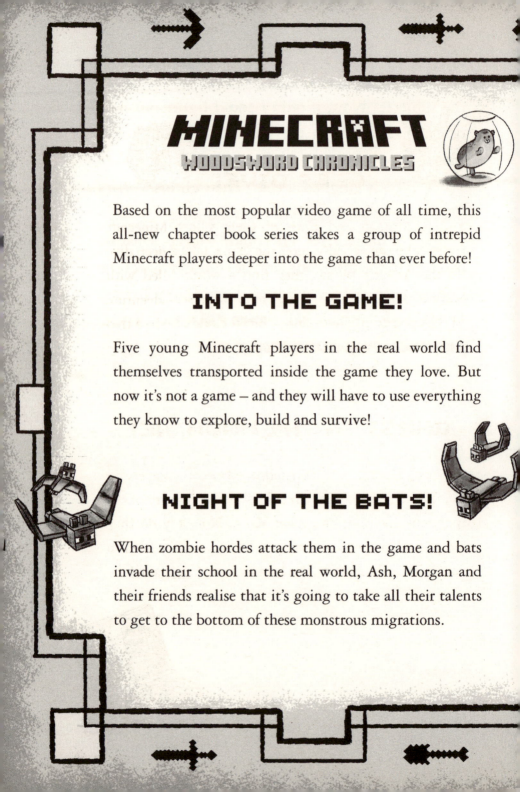

MINECRAFT
WOODSWORD CHRONICLES

Based on the most popular video game of all time, this all-new chapter book series takes a group of intrepid Minecraft players deeper into the game than ever before!

INTO THE GAME!

Five young Minecraft players in the real world find themselves transported inside the game they love. But now it's not a game – and they will have to use everything they know to explore, build and survive!

NIGHT OF THE BATS!

When zombie hordes attack them in the game and bats invade their school in the real world, Ash, Morgan and their friends realise that it's going to take all their talents to get to the bottom of these monstrous migrations.

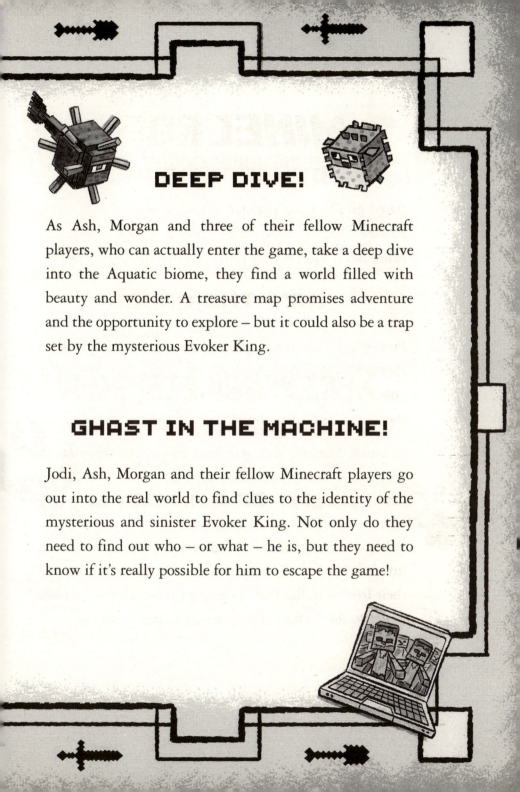

DEEP DIVE!

As Ash, Morgan and three of their fellow Minecraft players, who can actually enter the game, take a deep dive into the Aquatic biome, they find a world filled with beauty and wonder. A treasure map promises adventure and the opportunity to explore – but it could also be a trap set by the mysterious Evoker King.

GHAST IN THE MACHINE!

Jodi, Ash, Morgan and their fellow Minecraft players go out into the real world to find clues to the identity of the mysterious and sinister Evoker King. Not only do they need to find out who – or what – he is, but they need to know if it's really possible for him to escape the game!

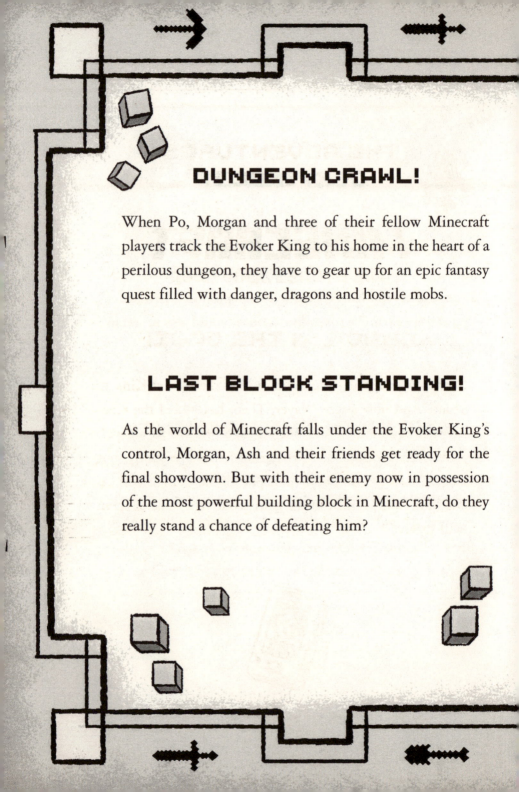

DUNGEON CRAWL!

When Po, Morgan and three of their fellow Minecraft players track the Evoker King to his home in the heart of a perilous dungeon, they have to gear up for an epic fantasy quest filled with danger, dragons and hostile mobs.

LAST BLOCK STANDING!

As the world of Minecraft falls under the Evoker King's control, Morgan, Ash and their friends get ready for the final showdown. But with their enemy now in possession of the most powerful building block in Minecraft, do they really stand a chance of defeating him?

THE ADVENTURES CONTINUE IN

MINECRAFT
THE STONESWORD SAGA

CRACK IN THE CODE!

Someone – or something – has turned the Evoker King to stone. And now a new player, Theo, has joined the team on their quest to return their former enemy to normal. Theo has modding skills that could come in handy, but does he have what it takes to be part of the team or will his meddling put a crack in the game code that none of them will survive?

MINECRAFT is a game about placing blocks and going on adventures. Build, play and explore across infinitely generated worlds of mountains, caverns, oceans, jungles and deserts. Defeat hordes of zombies, bake the cake of your dreams, venture to new dimensions or build a skyscraper. What you do in Minecraft is up to you.

Nick Eliopulos is a writer who lives in Brooklyn (as many writers do). He likes to spend half his free time reading and the other half gaming. He cowrote the Adventurers Guild series with his best friend and works as a narrative designer for a small video game studio. After all these years, endermen still give him the creeps.

Alan Batson is a British cartoonist and illustrator. His works include *Everything I Need to Know I Learned from a Star Wars Little Golden Book, Everything That Glitters is Guy!* and *Spider-Ham.* Being extremely fond of cubes and travel to exotic places, he has recently begun to lend his talents to several different books on adventures in the world of Minecraft.

Chris Hill is an illustrator living in Birmingham, England, with his wife and two daughters and has been loving it for twenty-five years! When he's not working, he spends time with his family and trying to tire out his dog on long walks. If there's any time left after that, he loves to go riding on his motorcycle, feeling the wind on his face while contemplating his next illustration adventure.